I'm the Moon in the Man
and I skip and play
all the star-bright night
and the live-long day.
Funny-bone, finger,
knuckle and knee,
follow your nose
and play with me.

A bouncing-on-the-knee,
joining-in,
make-'em-laugh,
happy times book of rhymes

To see the actions, go to:

www.allenandunwin.com/teaching/moonintheman.asp

For Lyn and Robyn and
Dame Nellie Melba Kindergarten

The Moon in the Man

Elizabeth Honey

ALLEN&UNWIN

First published in 2002

Allen & Unwin
83 Alexander Street
Crows Nest NSW 2065 Australia
Phone: (61 2) 8425 0100
Fax: (61 2) 9906 2218
Email: info@allenandunwin.com
Web: www.allenandunwin.com

National Library of Australia
Cataloguing-in-Publication entry:

Honey, Elizabeth, 1947– .
   The moon in the man.

   ISBN 1 86508 455 7 (hb)
   ISBN 1 86508 491 3 (pb)

   1. Nursery rhymes, Australian. I. Title.

398.8

Designed by Elizabeth Honey
Typeset in Comic Sans by Tou-Can Design
Printed in China by Leefung-Asco Printers Limited

10 9 8 7 6 5 4 3 2 1

Mud Soup

Mud soup
Mud soup
Fill up all the dishes
Mud soup
Mud soup
Try it—it's delicious!

Mighty Muscles

I'm a mighty muscle man
See my mighty muscles
I will wrestle anyone
From Bendigo to Brussels

I'm a mighty muscle girl
See my mighty muscles
Call me on your mobile
If you're ever in a tussle

I'm a mighty muscle tree
See my mighty muscles
When I wave my branches
You can hear my muscles rustle

Crash!

Lucky it was the eggs, not the legs!
Lucky it was the bread, not the head!
Lucky it was the pies, not the eyes!
Lucky it was the cheese, not the knees!

Zac Zucchini

Zac Zucchini
Drives a Lamborghini
Vroom *varoom*
Varoom vroom vroom

Donatella Deetle
Drives a little yellow Beetle
Dacka dacka dacka dacka
Dacka dacka dacka

Brian Boot
Drives a V8 ute
Boom boom boom boom boom boom boom boom
Barooom boom boom boom

Knucklehead Mike
Rides a mean dirt bike
Neeeeeeeyou neeeeeeeyou
Neeyou neeyou neeeeeyou

Vincenzo Rex
Drives a WRX
Boomp boomp boomp boomp
Boomp boomp boomp

Corrugations Loopy
Drives a bashed-up troupie
Brudda brudda brudda brudda
'Mind the kangaroo!'

Bruno da Brixer
Drives a ce-ment mixer
Hururururururururur
Hururururururur

Douglas Dopter
Flies a Bell helicopter
Chew chew chew chew chew chew chew chew
Chew chew chew chew chew

Popsy de Boyce
Drives a gold Rolls Royce
Prrrrrrrrrrrrrrrrrrrrrrrrrrrrr
rrrrrrrrrrrr 'Home James!'

Josephina Trampolina

Josephina Trampolina
She's a queena of the sky
Bounce a tumba, bounce a bumba
Bounce a million miles high

Josephina Trampolina
Loop da loopa in the sky
Bounce a tumba, bounce a bumba
Like a swallow she can fly

Josephina

trampoline

Stamping Joe

Hello, my name is Stamping Joe
And I work at the GPO
I stamp parcels big and small
My job is to stamp them all
I like stamping letters better
Stamp my stamp on every letter

My stamps are a splendid sight
In the corner on the right
When you see them now
You'll know
That they were stamped
By Stamping Joe

Hel - lo
my   name

big

small

a splendid sight

The Little
Little Little Boy

Once upon upon upon a time
In the land of Hobble-hobble-hoy
In a dark dark dark forest
Lived a little little little boy

One black black black night
Came a loud loud loud knock
An ugly ugly ugly monster
Like a nobbly nobbly nobbly rock

Crying giant giant giant tears
He gave a blood-curdling bellow
'There's an ouch ouch ouch in my eye.
Help help help me, little fellow.'

So the little little little boy
Had a quick quick quick think
'Yes yes yes, Mr Monster,
but promise not to blink.'

So the little little little boy
Swam in the crying crying crying eye
And with his tiny tiny tiny finger
Held the gritty gritty gritty grain high

Then the happy happy happy monster
Did a thump thump thump jig
'Thank thank you tiny fellow,
Little you saved me big.'

With his warm warm warm breath
He puff puffed him dry
Then set him down gently
And wave waved goodbye

Then the little little little boy
When the earth ceased to quake
Had a frothy frothy frothy coffee
And a teeny tiny weeny cake

How Do You Do?

Hello Mrs Lefty

       Hello Mrs Right

How are all your children?

       Very very polite

Good morning

       Good morning

Good afternoon

       Good afternoon

Good evening

       Good evening

Good night

       Good night

Woof! Woof! Woof!

You forgot your dog.

       Come *here*, Warthog!

Will he bite?

       He might!

Woof! Woof! Woof! Woof!

Morning! Morning!

Night! Night!

Your dog! Come here!

etc

Little Mr Big-toe

Little Mr Big-toe
In your wooden house you go
Little Mr Big-toe-too
Lives next door to you

Number Rumba

One sun
The day's begun

Two shoes
For kangaroos

Three trees
For catching the breeze

Four paws
Trotting indoors

Five lives
At the end of the drive

Six sticks
For sticky licks

Seven sevens
In seventh heaven

Eight plates
For William Gates

Nine vines
All entwined

Ten friends
Around the bend
Doing the
Number Rumba

Yellow Plastic Bucket

Here is a stick, a whicky-whacky stick
Pick it up and chuck it
In the yellow plastic bucket

Here is a stone, a rip-skip stone
Pick it up and chuck it
In the yellow plastic bucket

Here is a boy, a bonnie-bony boy
Pick it up...

Here is a girl, a girly-whirly girl
Pick it up...

Here is a bone, a telephone-y bone
Pick it up...

Here is a feather, a wickle-tickle feather
Pick it up...

Here is the end, a bendy-endy end
Full stop!

Bubble Wrap Rap

Snap pop pop
Pop pop snap
Dancing on
The bubble wrap

Snap pop pop
Pop pop hop
They all yell
At us to stop

Snap pop pop
We don't care
Dancing in
Our underwear!

Guess What?

I saw a car on a truck on a train
I ran to the crossing and I saw it again

I saw a bird on a cow on a hill
I ran by, but they stood still

I saw a hat on a girl on a gate
I saw a bird fly over an eight

I saw a horse on a king on a throne
I saw a cat in a dog-free zone

I saw a bottle on a post in the sea
I saw a fish but he didn't see me

I saw a giant dance on a wall
The sun went down, then he wasn't
    there at all

My Nose

I lost my nose in the sandpit
It just fell off my face
I've raked the sand
And sieved the sand
And dug all over the place
That's all very well
But I can't *smell*
It's done this before
Which is really
A bore
So if anyone knows
Where my naughty
Nose goes
Please put me
On track...
Oh there...

   It's *back!*

It's back!

Five Cents, Ten Cents

Five cents, ten cents
Fifty cents, a dollar
Here comes the dog
In his new flea collar
Here are the fish
Here are the chips
Here is the bollard
Where they tie up the ships

Worms in the compost
Wriggle, wriggle, wriggle
Kids in the corner
Giggle, giggle, giggle
Here are the fish
Here are the chips
Here is the bollard
Where they tie up the ships

Six
Five
Four, three, two
You for me
And me for you
One day
We'll run away
And live in a cave
On a moonlit bay . . .

Repeat first verse

Barker

Barker thinks he smells good
But we think Barker stinks
Down the path
And into the bath!
Now we think Barker smells good
But Barker thinks he stinks

My Computer

Here's my new computer
What a big bright screen!
Funniest screen saver
I've ever seen
Here is the mouse pad
Here is the mouse
This little mousie
Doesn't have a house
House keys?
Mouse keys?
Where are the ABCs?
Four fine rows
Right under my nose!

Tippety tap, tippety tap,
tippety tap *Clap clap*

Tippety tap, tippety tap,
tippety tap *Clap clap*

My computer's smashing!
Oops! *It crashed!*

new computer

tickle

screen saver

keys

mouse pad

bounce

Crazy Claps

A crazy clap
A lazy clap
A quack like a duck
A monster clap
A crocodile clap
A fairy clap for luck

Quack!
Quack.

monster

crocodile

fairy

Wavy Waves

A queen wave
A baby wave
A wave on the sea
A mad wave
A sad wave
A microwave on three *Ding!*

Min's Birthday

The girls planned a party
For Min on Saturday night
It was a secret party
So who did they invite?

Knock! Knock!   'Come in Tom Thumbkin'
Knock! Knock!   'Come in Pete Pointer'
Knock! Knock!   'Come in Luke Longman'
Knock! Knock!   'Come in Rob Ringo'
Knock! Knock!   'Come in Little Tim'

'Ssssh! Footsteps! Hide!'

They all hid under the table
'My birthday is sad,' cried Min
'There's nobody home!'

'Surprise! Surprise!
Let party time begin!'

Glitter and Glue

Glitter and glue
Glitter and glue
Magic me
Magic you
We look wonderful
We look new
See what a little bit
Of glitter can do!

All the Wild Wonders

For you my sweet babe
I wish fish in the sea
Birds in the trees
Tigers in jungles
And all the wild wonders
All the wild wonders
For you my sweet babe

For you my sweet babe
I wish carpets of wildflowers
Beetles and butterflies
Bright birds of paradise
And all the wild beauty
All the wild beauty
For you my sweet babe

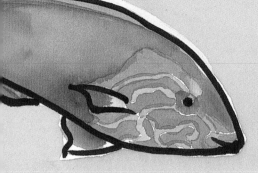

For you my sweet babe
I wish wind for the albatross
Clear flowing rivers
Forests of giants
And all the wild wonders
All the wild wonders
For you my sweet babe

For this wish to come true
We have much work to do
All the wild wonders
All the wild wonders
For you my sweet babe

Hug

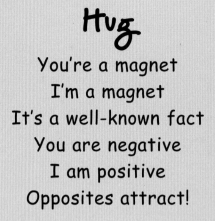

You're a magnet
I'm a magnet
It's a well-known fact
You are negative
I am positive
Opposites attract!